Sir NED and the NASTIES

Brett and David McKee

Andersen Press

The King lived in the castle on top of the hill.

He used to be happy but now he felt ill.

What made him so poorly? Terrible sounds.

Like wild screeching cats and howling old hounds.

The noises came from the deep dark of the wood.
The notorious Nasties, up to no good.
They scared the whole village
with their horrible drone
that came through the walls
and shook every home.

"Send me a knight, not afraid of a quest,"
commanded the King. "My bravest and best."
Sir Ned the Noble was the knight that he chose,
ready and eager to fight the King's foes.
"Don't worry," Sir Ned said. "I'll find who's to blame,
and then put an end to their ear-popping game."

He left for the woods where the wild wind was blowing
and there met a troll who asked, "Where are you going?"

"I seek the Nasties,
though it may take forever!"
"I know these woods well," said the Troll.
"Let's search together."

The trees were swaying
and the crows were crowing,
when a witch appeared asking,
"Where are you going?"

"We seek the Nasties
each one a crook."
"I know these woods well," said the Witch.
"I'll help you look."

By the twisted old bridge, a river was flowing.
A lurking wolf muttered, "Where are you going?"

"We seek the Nasties
and their secret lair."
"I know the place," said the Wolf.
"I'll take you there."

On tiptoe he led them to a well-hidden cave.
With a sign that said, "Enter here, if you be brave!"

Sir Ned whispered softly,
"The Nasties are near."
The others laughed at him,
"Yes, we're right here."

"We're the Nasties," they growled. "Welcome to our home.
You fell for our trick and now you're on your own."

They tied up Sir Ned and snarled in his face.
Then the Witch said, "You'll never escape from this place."
She waved her wand once, a fire burst into life.
The Wolf licked his lips, the Troll sharpened his knife.

They prodded and poked Ned,
then started to sing...

... the terrible noises
that upset the King!

"Ah," said Sir Ned,
"*This* I can fix.
When you sing together,
your voices must mix.
Listen to each other,
let the notes fill your heart.
The song will bring joy,
the magic will start."

Sir Ned sang a song which worked like a spell.
Changing bad into good and making all well.

The Nasties were grinning as they heard the tune.
The Troll joined in first, his voice as big as the moon.
The Witch got excited, her voice soaring higher.
Wolf hummed and drummed as they danced round the fire.

Their song sounded lovely,
not like before.
The King heard the music
and was happy once more.

"What fun," said the Nasties.
"Sir Ned, please don't go.
We sound good together –
let's put on a show."

Now they sing their songs up and down the land

and are famously known as 'Ned's Magic Band'!

There are no Nasties now, not in this wood.
That smell is the Stinkies who are up to no good.